The Rough-Face Girl

RAFE MARTIN

ILLUSTRATED BY
DAVID SHANNON

PUFFIN BOOKS

AUTHOR'S NOTE

To see good rewarded and evil punished, or justice, is rare. Stories, however, pass on the realities not of the everyday world but of the human heart. One way in which the universal yearning for justice has been kept alive is by the many tales of Cinderella. Indeed, some 1,500 or so versions of the basic Cinderella story-type have been recorded so far. In each, the cruel and thoughtless at last get their just reward, as do those who are kind and good.

The Rough-Face Girl, an Algonquin Indian Cinderella, is, in its original form, actually part of a longer and more complex traditional story. Brief as it is, however, The Rough-Face Girl remains one of the most magical, mysterious, and beautiful of all Cinderellas. Grown on native soil, its mystery is rooted in our own place. I am happy to pass it on to children and parents today.

To the enduring vision
of the earth's traditional peoples.
                                                    —R.M.

To Heidi, Bonne Bonne, and Donny.
                                                    —D.S.

Printed on recycled paper

Text copyright © 1992 by Rafe Martin. Illustrations copyright © 1992 by David Shannon. All rights reserved. This book, or parts thereof, may not be reproduced in any form without permission in writing from the publisher. A PaperStar Book, published in 1998 by The Putnam & Grosset Group, 200 Madison Avenue, New York, NY 10016. PaperStar is a registered trademark of The Putnam Berkley Group, Inc. The PaperStar logo is a trademark of The Putnam Berkley Group, Inc. Originally published in 1992 by G. P. Putnam's Sons. Published simultaneously in Canada. Printed in the United States of America. Book design by Gunta Alexander. The text was set in Veljovic. Library of Congress Cataloging-in-Publication Data Martin, Rafe, 1946- The rough-face girl / by Rafe Martin; illustrated by David Shannon. p. cm. Summary: In this Algonquin Indian version of the Cinderella story, the Rough-Face Girl and her two beautiful but heartless sisters compete for the affections of the Invisible Being. 1. Algonquin Indians—Legends. 2. Cinderella (Tale) [1. Algonquin Indians—Legends. 2. Indians of North America—Legends.] I. Shannon, David, 1959- ill. II. Title. E99.A349M37 1992 398.2'089973—dc20 [E] 91-2921 CIP AC ISBN 0-698-11626-7 10 9 8 7

Once, long ago, there was a village by the shores of Lake Ontario.

Off from the other wigwams of this village stood one great huge wigwam. Painted on its sides were pictures of the sun, moon, stars, plants, trees, and animals. And inside this wigwam there was said to live a very great, rich, powerful, and supposedly handsome Invisible Being. However, no one could see him, except his sister, who lived there too.

Many women wanted to marry this Invisible Being, but his sister said, "Only the one who can see him can marry him."

Now, in this village there lived a poor man who had three daughters. The two older daughters were cruel and hard-hearted, and they made their youngest sister sit by the fire and feed the flames. When the burning branches popped, the sparks fell on her.

In time, her hands became burnt and scarred. Her arms too became rough and scarred. Even her face was marked by the fire, and her beautiful long black hair hung ragged and charred.

And those two older sisters laughed at her saying, "Ha! You're ugly, you Rough-Face Girl!" And they made her life very lonely and miserable, indeed.

One day these two older sisters went to their father and said, "Father, give us some necklaces. Give us some new buckskin dresses. Give us some pretty beaded moccasins. We're going to marry the Invisible Being."

So their father gave them these things. Dressed in their finest, the two girls marched through the village. All the people pointed and stared. "Look at those beautiful girls," they said. "Surely they shall marry the Invisible Being!"

And if those two girls were proud and hard-hearted before, they were even prouder now. They walked haughtily through the village. At last they came to the wigwam of the Invisible Being. And there was his sister, waiting.

"Why have you come?" she asked.

"We want to marry the Invisible Being," they answered. "That's why we're here."

"If you want to marry my brother," she replied, "you have to have seen him. Tell me, have you seen the Invisible Being?"

"Of course we've seen him," they insisted. "Can't you see how pretty we are? Can't you see the beautiful clothes we wear? Oh yes, anyone can tell that we've truly seen the Invisible Being."

"All right," she said quietly, "if you think you've seen him, then tell me, WHAT'S HIS BOW MADE OF?" And suddenly her voice was swift as lightning and strong as thunder!

"H–his b–b–bow?" they stammered in surprise. "His, uh, bow? We know! We know!" But turning desperately to one another, they whispered, "What shall we say? Let's say it's the oak tree." So they said, "It's the great oak tree."

"No!" said the sister of the Invisible Being. "NO!" Oh, she saw at once how they lied. "Tell me," she continued, "if you think you've seen my brother the Invisible Being, then WHAT'S THE RUNNER OF HIS SLED MADE OF?"

"Uh, we know, we know!" cried those two sisters. But whispering feverishly again they wondered, "What shall we say? What shall we say? Let's say it's the green willow branch."

"NO!" said the sister when she heard. "NO! You have not seen my brother. Now go home."

"Just test us fairly!" they exclaimed. "We've seen him. Just don't ask us all these silly questions!"

"All right," said the sister of the Invisible Being, "come with me."

And she took them back to the great wigwam and sat them in the seats furthest from the entrance, the guests' seats. Soon they heard footsteps coming along the path. Then Something stepped inside. Though they heard breathing, the two sisters still couldn't see a thing. Suddenly a great bow and a beaded quiver of arrows appeared in the air and were set down. But though those two girls sat there, their eyes wide, all through that night they never saw a thing more. And in the morning they had to go home, ashamed.

The next day the Rough-Face Girl went to her father and said, "Father, may I please have some beads? May I please have a new buckskin dress and some pretty moccasins? I am going to marry the Invisible Being, for, wherever I look, I see his face."

But her father sighed. "Daughter," he said, "I'm sorry. I have no beads left for you, only some little broken shells. I have no buckskin dress, and as for moccasins, all I have left are my own old, worn, cracked, and stretched-out pair from last year. And they're much too big."

But she said, "Whatever you can spare, I can use."

So he gave her these things.

Then she found dried reeds and, taking the little broken shells, she strung a necklace. She stripped birch bark from the dead trees and made a cap, a dress, and leggings. Then, with a sharp piece of bone, she carved in the bark pictures of the sun, moon, stars, plants, trees, and animals.

She went down to the lakeshore and soaked the moccasins in the water until they grew soft. Then she molded them to her feet. But they were still too big and they *flap, flap, flapped* like ducks' feet as she walked. Then all of the people came out of their wigwams. They pointed and stared. "Look at that ugly girl!" they laughed. "Look at her strange clothes! Hey! Hey! Hey! Go home you ugly girl! You'll never marry the Invisible Being!"

But the Rough-Face Girl had faith in herself and she had courage. She didn't turn back. She just kept walking right through the village.

As she walked on she saw the great beauty of the earth and skies spreading before her.

And truly she alone, of all in that village, saw in these things
the sweet yet awesome face of the Invisible Being.

At last she came to the lakeshore just as the sun was sinking behind the hills and the many stars came glittering out like a fiery veil in the darkening sky overhead.

And there, standing by the water's edge, was the sister of the Invisible Being, waiting.

Now, the sister of the Invisible Being was a wise woman. When she looked at you she didn't see just your face or your hair or clothes. No. When she looked at you she would look you right in the eyes and she could see all the way down to your heart. And she could tell if you had a good, kind heart or a cold, hard, and cruel one. And when she looked at the Rough-Face Girl she saw at once that, though her skin was scarred, her hair burnt, her clothes strange, she had a beautiful, kind heart. And so she welcomed her dearly saying, "Ah, my sister, why have you come?"

And the Rough-Face Girl replied, "I have come to marry the Invisible Being."

"Ah," said the sister very gently now. "If you want to marry him, you have to have seen him. Tell me, have you seen my brother the Invisible Being?"

And the Rough-Face Girl said, "Yes."

"All right, then," said the sister, "if you have seen him, tell me WHAT'S HIS BOW MADE OF?"

And the Rough-Face Girl said, "His bow? Why, it is the great curve of the Rainbow."

"AHHH!" exclaimed the sister in excitement. "Tell me," she asked, "if you have seen my brother the Invisible Being—WHAT'S THE RUNNER OF HIS SLED MADE OF?"

And the Rough-Face Girl, looking up into the night sky, said, "The runner of his sled? Why, it is the Spirit Road, the Milky Way of stars that spreads across the sky!"

"AHHHHHH!" cried the sister in wonder and delight. "You have seen him! Come with me!"

And taking the Rough-Face Girl by the hand, she led her back to the great wigwam and sat her in the seat next to the entrance, the wife's seat.

Then they heard footsteps coming along the path, closer and closer. The entrance flap of the wigwam lifted up, and in stepped the Invisible Being.

And when he saw her sitting there he said, "At last we have been found out." Then, smiling kindly, he added, "And oh, my sister, but she is beautiful."

And his sister said, "Yes."

The sister of the Invisible Being then gave the Rough-Face Girl the finest of buckskin robes and a necklace of perfect shells. "Now bathe in the lake," she said, "and dress in these."

So the Rough-Face Girl bathed in the waters of the lake. Suddenly all the scars vanished from her body. Her skin grew smooth again and her beautiful black hair grew in long and glossy as a raven's wing. Now anyone could see that she was, indeed, beautiful. But the Invisible Being and his sister had seen that from the start.

Then at last the Rough-Face Girl and the Invisible Being
were married.
They lived together in great gladness and were never parted.